DAVID
and
the
ICE ELF

For my mother, who was kind enough to look the other
way when I was conversing with my elves. And still does.
W. M.
To my son, who reminded me of winter's magical beauty.
M. H.

DAVID and the ICE ELF

by Winifred Morris
illustrated by Maureen Hyde

Atheneum   1988   New York

High in the highest mountains, where the snow stays on all through the year, the ice elves live in caves under the snow. And when the sun shines so that melting snow trickles into their homes, they hide in their deepest chambers. For they, too, might melt in the sun.

They have lived there so long that they tell stories of huge, winged animals without feathers that flew overhead. They tell stories of lizard monsters that prowled the lowlands. And they tell stories of wood elves who also lived in the forests of the lowlands.

In the winter, when the snow reaches down the mountains, the ice elves journey down the mountains, too, under the protection of the snow. They are hoping to visit their lowland cousins, but for many years they have found no one to visit.

Now fewer and fewer of them make the winter journey. And some of the younger ones laugh when they hear stories of wood elves. They don't believe they exist. They don't believe they ever existed.

Xinni laughed when his father told him they were going to travel down the mountain. He laughed when his mother asked him to pack for the journey. But he didn't laugh when he and his family left their cozy cave and started on their way. He wanted to stay home with his friends and his toys.

"Do we have to?" he asked his father. "I've seen wood elves. I've seen pictures of them in books. And if you ask me, they look just like us. Only they're kind of furry."

But his father insisted that wood elves were a wonder to see, even though he, too, had seen them only in books.

"You'll be glad I took you to see them," he said. "And you'll be amazed! I've been told that when you get really close to them—when you really get a good look at them— they look just like us! Only they're kind of furry."

They had to tunnel their way through the snow. Xinni got very tired of it all.

Xinni's father got tired, too. He got tired when something huge poked its shiny black nose into their tunnel one day. He got tired when the sun shone so brightly that clumps of snow falling from the trees sounded like thunder all around them. Their tunnel collapsed in several places, and Xinni's father spent three days shouting at Xinni and running back and forth with rocks and twigs and pine cones. Xinni tried to stay out of the way and wished he were home.

But a few days later, a fresh snowfall made traveling so much easier that they made their camp early in the day. And Xinni's father said, "I bet we'll see the wood elves soon."

"I'm going to play in the snow," said Xinni. "Tell me when you find them."

Not far away, someone else was pleased with the new snow. It meant the school bus wouldn't be able to come. David wasn't going to have to go to school. Instead he could play with his friends and his toys.

But his father had another idea. "Get your boots on," he said. "I'm going to take you to see the elk!"

"Do we have to?" asked David. "I've seen elk. Last summer I saw a whole bunch of them."

"Those were just dots on a hill," said his father. "They were so far away they could have been elephants and you wouldn't have known the difference."

"I didn't think they were elephants," said David.

But his father insisted that elk were a wonder to see, even though he, too, had seen them only from a distance. He knew where the Game Commission was feeding them hay. He knew exactly when the Game Commission brought the hay each day, and, of course, so did the elk.

"You'll be glad I took you to see them," he said. "And you'll be amazed! We'll be so close to them, they'll look so big to you, you'll think they're elephants!"

But on their way to see the elk, the truck slid into a ditch. David's father spent two hours yelling at David and running around with a shovel, a jack, a hand-operated winch, and a whole lot of tree branches. David tried to stay out of the way and wished he were home.

By the time they got to the place where the Game Commission was feeding the elk, all they found were tire tracks and some very big, round footprints.

David's father scowled at the trampled hay. David tossed a snowball at him. But that didn't work out very well, so David decided he'd better leave his father alone for awhile.

Xinni saw David before David saw Xinni. Xinni thought David was rather big for a wood elf, but he couldn't be sure.

When David saw Xinni, there was no question in his mind that this was no elk.

David came closer.
Xinni popped back under the snow.
David came closer.
Xinni just had to take another look.

"David, where are you? We might as well go home," yelled David's father.

"Dad, look!"

But David's father, who was puffing when he appeared, looked all around and didn't see any elk.

"Over there! Don't you see it!"

"David, come on. The way things are going, we'll probably get stuck again trying to get out of here."

As he hustled David back to the truck, he almost stepped on Xinni.

Just in time, Xinni's father pulled Xinni back into the safety of the snow. He had found no wood elves and was ready to go home.

But Xinni didn't want to leave now!

Neither did David!

David knew he had seen something, even if his father hadn't. Maybe his father didn't see the way the needles of the trees were feathered with tiny crystals either. Or the way the lacy heads of the dried grass looked like fresh blooms. He didn't seem to have noticed that the angle of the afternoon sun was making everything look as if it were dusted with diamonds.

David's father was tightening the chains on the truck. What he said was, "This has been a whole lot of work for nothing."

David didn't feel that way anymore, but he didn't try to argue. For he had spotted Xinni again, now grinning bravely not far away.

But maybe his father would be right about one thing. Maybe, the way things were going, they would be lucky enough to get stuck again trying to get out of there.

Atheneum, Macmillan Publishing Company, 866 Third Avenue, New York, NY 10022
Collier Macmillan Canada, Inc.
First Edition
Printed in Japan

10   9   8   7   6   5   4   3   2   1

Library of Congress Cataloging-in-Publication Data

Morris, Winifred. David and the ice elf/by Winifred Morris; illustrated by Maureen Hyde.
—1st edition.   p.   cm.
Summary: Unwillingly taken for outings in the snow by their
fathers, a boy and an ice elf meet by chance.
ISBN 0-689-31428-0   [1. Elves—Fiction.   2. Winter—Fiction.]   I. Hyde, Maureen, ill.
II. Title.   PZ7.M82923Dav   1988 [E]—dc19
87-27799   CIP   AC